TO: MATHEW

MERRY CHRISTMAS

Michael J. Snopla

11/19/88

A Deer Love Story

A
DEER
LOVE
STORY

Michael J. Smajda

VANTAGE PRESS
New York / Los Angeles / Chicago

Illustrated by Christina Nair

FIRST EDITION

Published by Vantage Press, Inc.
516 West 34th Street, New York, New York 10001

Manufactured in the United States of America
ISBN: 0-533-07680-3

To my wife, Jean, and my children, Jean Marie, Mary Ellen, Kay, Michelle, and Diana, and to my grandchildren

A Deer Love Story

I

One very wintery Christmastime,
Far up north where the reindeer dwell,
There wandered a lonely orphan fawn,
And her name was Estherell.

Since the very day she became an orphan,
She had been searching all over to find
Someone who would give her a loving home,
But not as yet had she found someone kind.

All the while she roamed the Northlands,
The cold winds from each direction would
    storm,
Shivering and shaking poor Estherell's
    frame
So that it was hard for her to keep warm.

For all she wore were scraps of rags,
Which hardly covered her body quite lean
And were randomly scattered all about her,
That nearly all of her spots could be seen.

At last she climbed a very high peak,
And guess what her eyes did see?
Window-lit homes with chimneys still
    puffing.
Estherell's heart was filled with glee!

She could feel the warmth of their fireplaces
As she pranced closer toward this site.
Already her mouth was tasting sweet
    morsels
She soon would be eating this night.

As Estherell meekly entered the village,
She felt ashamed and somewhat distressed.
Maybe she would not even be welcomed,
Since like a beggar she was truly dressed.

But before she could tidy up her garments,
Shadowy figures from the doorways
    appeared.
And as they all gathered around her,
She sensed they were strangers to be feared.

They greeted her coldly and they looked very
    mean,
These creatures that occupied the street.
They all were ugly, jeering implings.
They frightened her from her head to her
    feet.

When one of them growled what she wanted,
And before she had a chance to reply,
One little urchin threw a tiny snowball,
Which painfully struck her above her right
    eye.

Then taunting songs they started singing,
And awful pranks they upon her played,
Till soon tears appeared from her eyelids.
My, was poor Estherell ever dismayed.

As she nursed the bruises they had given her,
She heard the implings unanimously agree,
Despite who she was or what she was
     wanting,
Alive she would never leave their cruel city.

Upon hearing such plans to harm her,
She escaped and ran fast into the night,
Till no more could she see the imps' village
And was safely far from its site.

As the evening grew older and colder,
Estherell's tired body knew what was best,
And upon luckily finding an empty cave,
Here Estherell decided to rest.

Thinking not of the terrible imps anymore,
She began to dwell on this hopeful prayer:
Simply, that somebody good and kindly
Might still give her a home somewhere.

Now the spot where she lay thawed a bit.
Soon her eyes grew heavy with sleep.
Though she was dreaming of food and of
    warmth,
These thoughts made Estherell sob and
    weep.

For she dreamt the food she was biting into
Was spitefully biting her back!
And dreamt a fire full of impish flames
Kept pinching her each time they would
    crack!

Frightened by this dream, she screamed
        aloud,
Awakening from this horrible nightmare
Just in time for her ears to keenly hear
A distant sobbing fill the night air.

II

A misfortune had come to Santa's land!
Rudolph's nose was not shining bright!
What was poor Santa going to do?
Who would direct him on Christmas night?

Santa looked and searched through every
    book
To find a cure for Rudolph's nose.
He read and read till the pages blurred,
But no cure would his books disclose.

Still Santa did not give up hope;
He asked for help in every town.
"Whoever shall light up Rudolph's nose,"
He declared, "forever shall be renowned!"

Santa took Rudolph everywhere
And had him try every potion and pill,
But no one knew the magic cure
That would light up Rudolph's nose at will.

Naturally, Santa began to worry some;
Christmas Eve was not far away.
He was not sure he could travel safely
Without Rudolph's nose to guide his sleigh.

And poor Rudolph, too, was very sad.
Since he was of no help to Santa anymore,
He went off alone, sobbing and crying,
Because his nose would not glow as before.

Along the way he met this fawn,
Who, too, was roaming the same sad trail.
He learned the fawn was lonely and
    orphaned
And that she called herself Estherell.

Estherell told him all of her troubles
And Rudolph told Estherell all of his.
Soon they both felt sorry for each other
And no more did they each other quiz.

Now there were two unhappy reindeer
Wandering over the Northland's snow,
Both were feeling helpless and worthless,
And both had no special place to go.

After several days of wandering,
Both got to know each other well.
Estherell grew fond of Rudolph
And Rudolph grew fond of Estherell.

Together they cared for each other,
Like everybody is supposed to do.
And whenever they found any berries,
They always shared them equally, too.

Now one of their morning journeys
Led them up a very steep hill,
And it was here that orphan Estherell
Lost her footing and took a bad spill.

Startled Rudolph could not stop her,
As he had pranced too far ahead.
Watching her go tumbling down the hillside
Was, for poor Rudolph, a sight to dread.

As he grievingly stood looking downward
At Estherell's motionless body below,
It suddenly came upon little Rudolph
How much he really loved her so.

As he descended the slippery pathway
To where the snow bed had halted her fall,
He wished he had helped her up the steep
    path.
Then this would not have happened to her
    at all.

When he reached her, he tried to arouse her.
Tho' she was breathing, she made no sound.
There wasn't a thing that he could do for her
'Cept wait and lie beside her on the cold
    ground.

Estherell miraculously began to awaken.
And discovering all her senses still were fine,
She joyfully kissed the lips of dear Rudolph.
And as she did, do you know what began to
    shine?

"My nose! My nose!" pointed Rudolph
    excitedly.
"Estherell, look what happened to my nose!
You made my nose light up, Estherell!
Ever since you kissed me, my nose now
    glows!"

Strange as it was to the two of them,
What Rudolph cheered to her was true!
It was Estherell's lips that made his nose
    glow.
Now if goodly Santa Claus only knew!

Rudolph decided to return to Santa's Land.
Now there was no reason for him to roam.
Now he could guide Santa Claus Christmas
    night,
And Santa would gladly give Estherell a good
    home.

Rudolph and Estherell had not gone far,
When there appeared in the skies far off,
A red-clothed man gliding directly toward
    them.
It was Santa searching for Rudolph!

"I never would have found you, Rudolph,
If it had not been for your beaming nose!
My! How did you get it to glow again?"
Their secret to Santa they began to disclose.

He laughed as they told him about their
    kissing,
And his fleet of reindeer laughed with him,
    too.
He smiled, "Your nose must be like my
    flashlights,
Always needing recharging like flashlights
    do!"

Then Santa turned to the orphan and said,
"Since you cured the nose of Rudolph,
    Estherell,
No more will you be a lonely orphan deer,
At my home forever you shall always dwell!"

Now that Rudolph's nose was again shining
    brightly,
And Santa had Rudolph to guide him
    Christmas night,
And Estherell finally found her loving, sweet
    home,
All three boarded the sleigh for their
    homeward flight.

Then up and away the happy threesome flew,
For this Christmas night they had things to
        do,
Such as give out toys to good little boys
And good little girls like all of you.

But the best gift of all Santa saved for last
It was for the world all over to share.
He announced the marriage of two reindeer
Whose love for each other he found quite
     rare.

And before Christmas evening ended,
While showering, ricelike snowflakes fell,
Santa wedded these two forever,
Good Rudolph and sweet Estherell.